THE DARKEST HOUR

SOLAK
SCOURGE OF
THE SEA

With special thanks to Michael Ford

To Billy Thorne

www.beastquest.co.uk

ORCHARD BOOKS
Carmelite House
50 Victoria Embankment
London EC4Y 0DZ

A Paperback Original
First published in Great Britain in 2013

Beast Quest is a registered trademark of Beast Quest Limited
Series created by Beast Quest Limited, London

Text © Beast Quest Limited 2013
Inside illustrations by Pulsar Estudio (Beehive Illustration) © Beast
Quest Limited 2013. Cover by Steve Sims © Beast Quest Limited 2013

A CIP catalogue record for this book is available from
the British Library.

ISBN 978 1 40832 396 0

7 9 10 8 6

Printed and bound by CPI Group (UK) Ltd, Croydon, CR0 4YY

MIX
Paper from
responsible sources
FSC® C104740

The paper and board used in this book are made from wood
from responsible sources.

Orchard Books is an imprint of Hachette Children's Group
and published by The Watts Publishing Group Limited,
an Hachette UK company.

www.hachette.co.uk

SOLAK
SCOURGE OF
THE SEA

BY ADAM BLADE

ORCHARD

TION

THE RAINBOW JUNGLE

Dear Reader,

My hand shakes as I write. You find us in our hour of greatest peril.

My master Aduro has been snatched away. The kingdom is on its knees. Not one, but two enemies circle our shores – Kensa, the banished witch, has returned from Henkrall. With her stalks Sanpao, the Pirate King. Strange magic is afoot, stirring not just in Avantia but all the kingdoms, and I sense new Beasts lurking.

Only Tom and Elenna stand in the way of certain destruction. Can they withstand the awful test that will surely come? This time, courage alone may have to be enough.

Yours, in direst straits,

Daltec the apprentice

PROLOGUE

Freya gripped the hard ridge of shell behind Krabb's head, as the Beast skimmed across the water, throwing spray from his legs. After Taladon's funeral, she had returned home to Gwildor. There could be no rest for a Mistress of the Beasts. The kingdom had to be patrolled at all costs.

As Krabb slowly swam through the calm turquoise water, Freya lifted her face to the warm sun. A niggling doubt crept into the back of her mind.

How was Tom faring in Henkrall? Aduro had sent word of her son's latest Quest, but no details of the dangers he faced...

She opened her eyes when she heard Krabb's pincers clacking anxiously. "Yes, I feel something too," she muttered, feeling the hair on her arms stand on end.

A strange energy thrummed in the air and the sea dimmed from green-blue to grey. Krabb tensed beneath her as the waters became choppy, smacking against his armoured flanks. A low grinding sound that seemed to come from everywhere and nowhere filled her ears, as the sky above was stained with black, rolling clouds.

In the distance, in the direction of Avantia, lightning flashed, fork after fork stabbing downwards.

Thunder rumbled across the sky like a thousand galloping warhorses. Even Freya felt a tickle of fear.

Only Evil magic could produce lightning like that, she thought.

Krabb twisted in the water, his eyes swivelling and his claws raised, braced for an attack. Freya saw that he was looking at a dark shape swimming beneath the chopping waves. It was coming straight for them. She drew her sword.

The approaching creature broke the surface and Freya saw it was a giant shark, with a sleek silvery body and a gaping mouth big enough to swallow a person whole. Its eyes were like polished jet orbs, set high and far back on its jutting head. Its body glowed blue, shifting to violet and indigo like a slick of oil in the sun,

and its fins were lined with blades
of serrated bone, like jagged teeth.

"Who sent you?" Freya muttered,
her grip tightening on her sword.
This menace wasn't going to get past
them, even if the Mistress of the

Beasts died defending her kingdom.

At the last moment, the Beast veered in the water and swam in the opposite direction, sinking out of sight.

"After him, Krabb!" she said, locking her arms tight and just barely managing to hang on as the Good Beast surged through the water in pursuit. But as Freya scanned the ocean, there was no sign of their foe. What she saw were hundreds of other sea dwellers massing around Krabb's legs in panic – rainbow-coloured fish and pulsing octopuses. Smaller sharks swam in circles, ignoring fish that would normally be their prey. Other sea animals that Freya didn't recognise at all were also swarming – jellyfish with blue hearts and transparent bodies, fish shaped like

puffed up balls with jutting spines,
and hundreds of five-legged sea
spiders.

These creatures don't belong here, she
thought, almost losing her balance as
Krabb jolted to a sudden stop in the

water. She looked up and gasped.

It can't be…

To the east she could clearly see the Avantian shoreline. But her eyes must have been playing tricks on her – Avantia was two day's hard sailing away from Gwildor.

She cast a glance back. Sure enough, Gwildor's dark, tree-lined coast was also near. A strong swimmer could cover the distance between them in just a few hours.

"What evil magic has drawn entire kingdoms through the sea?" she murmured. Krabb let out a low moan of anxiety and she patted his shell.

Whatever trouble was coming their way, they'd have to try to be ready…

CHAPTER ONE

ADURO ON TRIAL

Tom tried again to insert the ruby among the other jewels on his belt, but it wouldn't stay in place. He'd won it on his Quest against Torgor the Minotaur, and it gave him the power to communicate with any Beast, good or evil. For some reason, the ruby had fallen out when he and Elenna had travelled back from Henkrall via the Lightning Path. Sighing, he slipped the jewel into his tunic for safekeeping. *Perhaps Aduro could put it back one day*, he thought. *If we ever see our friend again…*

"There must be some way we can help him!" said Elenna. She was talking to a gathering of Avantian knights.

The two of them stood in front of King Hugo in his throne room. At their side was Daltec, Aduro's young wizard apprentice. On their return from Henkrall, Aduro had been arrested by the Circle of Wizards and charged with the crime of using forbidden Lightning Magic.

The King looked at each of them in turn. "The Circle is made up of the most powerful wizards from every kingdom," he said. "Not even I can overrule them."

"But Aduro was using the magic for the right reason," said Tom. "Without it, we couldn't have pursued the sorceress Kensa to Henkrall."

"And Avantia would have been in mortal danger," Elenna added.

The King shook his head sadly. "There's nothing we can do."

Tom turned from the throne and stared out of the window over the palace courtyard. Masons and carpenters were still at work on repairs to the dungeon entrance. It had been destroyed when Kensa broke Sanpao the Pirate King out of jail.

Tom clenched his fist. *It's up to me to bring them both to justice once more.* But without his wizard friend's help, the new Quest would be ten times harder.

"There must be a way we can talk to Aduro," he said, turning to Daltec.

"My master must stand trial first," the young wizard said. "He'll be questioned by the Circle and must make his defence. But using the Lightning Path is a serious crime."

"When is this trial taking place?" asked Hugo. "Perhaps we can stand as witnesses?"

Daltec's eyes dropped towards the stone floor. "The trial has already begun."

"Already?" said Tom, surprised. He pointed at Daltec. "Can you magic us there?"

Daltec shrank back. "I'm not sure I should. It's a matter for the Wizards to…"

Tom strode towards the apprentice, anger boiling in his chest. "Aduro

needs us!" he snapped.

Elenna placed a hand on his arm.
"Perhaps Daltec's right," she said.
"Breaking the rules is what got us
into all this trouble in the first place.
I know it's not like me to say it, but
maybe we should be more cautious
now."

Tom felt his fury cool down, but

he wasn't ready to give up. "After everything Aduro has done for us, I won't let him rot in some prison. I'm begging you to help us, Daltec."

The apprentice looked at his feet. "I don't know what to do," he admitted.

"Let me make this easier," said King Hugo, standing up. "I order you, as a subject of Avantia, to help Tom. I will answer for any trouble."

Daltec looked up and nodded. "Then I will aid you as best I can," he said. "But my magic will only allow you to watch the trial. No one will be able to see or hear you – which means that you cannot speak up. No matter what happens, you will not be able to interfere."

Tom felt his frustration bubble up again. "Watching will have to be enough," he said.

Daltec drew a crystal orb from his robes and held it aloft. His lips moved with a silent incantation. "Come closer," he said.

As they approached, Tom couldn't help staring into the orb. Cloudy patterns swirled beneath the surface, forming images. He saw a round chamber, with columns lining the walls. Several men and women in bright robes and pointed hats sat in the grand room.

Elenna gasped. "Is that…?"

"Keep watching," said Daltec. The crystal seemed to crack and open like the petals of a blooming flower, flooding the throne room with violet light. Tom blinked and brought his hands to his eyes. When he looked again, King Hugo and the throne room were gone.

Daltec's magic had worked. Tom and Elenna were standing behind a column at the edge of the Wizard Court.

The chamber was perfectly circular. Everything inside it was rounded too, from the patterns on the walls to the stools and tables. On a raised semi-circular bench sat three ancient-looking Wizards in dark green robes. *They must be the most senior Wizards*, Tom thought.

The chamber echoed with muttered words as the Wizards leant their heads close to one another.

Two seats, side by side, were empty, and Tom squinted to read the engraved names on the tables.

Malvel. Velmal.

He gasped. Even Evil Wizards had

once sat on the Circle! Then he noticed a third vacant chair…

Kensa.

"Silence!" boomed one of the three senior Wizards. The others obeyed at once and the echo of their voices faded.

Tom glanced around the column and saw Aduro kneeling, head bowed, in the centre of the Court. His hands were bound behind his back by a glowing chain of emeralds. Tom felt his heart lurch in dread and pity. The old Wizard's robes were torn and filthy, his beard unkempt.

"What have they done to him?" Elenna whispered.

"I don't know," Tom said, "but I'm going to make them pay for it." He tried to draw his sword, and found he couldn't pull it from the scabbard.

Daltec's magic! he realised. *He said we wouldn't be able to interfere.*

One of the three senior Wizards rose from his seat. Tom saw that his name was written in front of his seat: *Jezrin*. The deep wrinkles of his face twisted around a sour, cruel mouth as he glared down at Aduro. *Like an old vulture*, Tom thought. *It looks as though this Wizard will decide the fate of my friend. He must be the Judge.*

"You have been accused of the gravest crimes," said the Judge to Aduro. "How do you plead?"

Tom waited for Aduro to stand up and defend himself. But his friend stayed kneeling and didn't even lift his head as he croaked one word...

"Guilty."

CHAPTER TWO

A DANGEROUS BARGAIN

The Wizards broke out in muttered conversations.

"No!" shouted Tom. "He's innocent!"

He leapt out from behind the column but Elenna caught his arm. "There's nothing you can do, Tom," she said. "Remember what Daltec said."

Sure enough, none of the Wizards had heard Tom's shout, or seen him lunge forward. He was invisible.

The Wizard in the green robes smiled. "Will anyone in the Circle speak for this criminal?" His eyes travelled around the room, but none of the other Wizards spoke a word. "No one?" said the Judge. "What about our uninvited guests?"

"He can see us!" Elenna whispered.

"Of course I can see you," said the Judge, his cold gaze resting on Tom. "Your magic is pathetic."

All the other Wizards turned in their seats, looking in the same direction. But from their blank stares, Tom suspected only the Judge could see them.

"Tom... Elenna..." said a weak voice. He saw Aduro trying to stand,

looking at him with watery eyes.
"You shouldn't have come here."

So only two Wizards could see
them. *They must be the most powerful
in the circle*, Tom thought.

Murmurs broke out among the
others.

"What's happening?"

"Who's he talking to?"

The Judge let out a deafening
clap with his hands, and suddenly
gasps and shouts rang out from the
gathered sorcerers. Dozens of pairs
of eyes widened and Tom realised
they weren't invisible any more. He
instinctively reached for his sword.

Wizards shot up from their seats,
levelling staffs and gnarled wooden
wands in their direction. Elenna
had an arrow at her bowstring in an
instant.

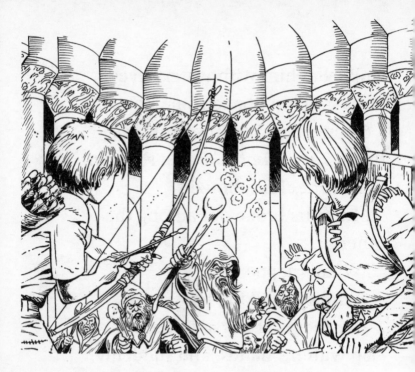

Even with all the skills of a Master
of the Beasts, Tom realised he was
at a severe disadvantage against so
many Wizards.

One wrong move and we'll be on the
receiving end of some nasty magic, he
thought.

"Lower your bow," he said.

Elenna looked at him uncertainly,
but she let the bowstring slacken and

replaced the arrow in her quiver.
Tom raised his own hands.

"A wise decision," said the Judge.
"Fear not, fellow Wizards, these pesky
children are merely spies." He spat
the last word.

"We came to help our friend,"
said Elenna.

"Send them back," begged
Aduro from the floor. "They don't
understand what they're doing."

Why doesn't he want our help? Tom
wondered.

The Judge raised an eyebrow. "I
think they understand perfectly well,"
he said. "They think they can meddle
in the affairs of their betters. Well,
let's see what they have to say."

The courtroom fell silent again.
Tom stepped forwards until he stood
beside Aduro.

"Leave!" said the loyal old Wizard. "There's nothing you can do."

Tom stared at his friend, seeing a hopeless look in his eyes.

"Aduro was trying to do good," Tom told the Judge. "Kensa was the enemy, surely you can see that? She had to be battled somehow."

"He broke an ancient law," said the Judge. "He committed one of the gravest crimes."

Tom could hardly believe what he was hearing. He pointed to Malvel's empty chair. "Malvel committed grave crimes," he said.

"Malvel is not on trial here," said the Judge. "Aduro is."

"Heroes make mistakes," said Tom. "But Aduro's motive was good."

"A noble effort," said the Judge, "but Aduro's intentions do not matter.

The fact is that Kensa and Sanpao are now loose in Avantia. Your kingdom is in greater danger than ever because of Aduro's use of the Lightning Path. Besides, he has already pleaded guilty. We shall proceed to sentencing—"

"Wait!" said Elenna, rushing to Tom's side. "There must be some way we can repay the wrong."

The Judge's eyes narrowed. "What can two children do for the Circle of Wizards?"

Tom bristled, but held his tongue. Losing his temper wouldn't help. "I've been helping Wizards for a long time now," he said. "I've earned some trust."

"Is that so?" said the Judge, his eyes blazing.

If this doesn't work, Aduro is finished, thought Tom.

"The Circle should let us go after the real villains," he said, pointing to one of the empty seats. "Kensa is the enemy. Surely she is the bigger prize. If we can capture her for you, will you let Aduro go free?"

A few of the assembled Wizards looked on, nodding with approval. Others muttered under their breaths.

"The Avantian boy's right," said one Wizard, whose long red beard spilled over his silver robes.

The Judge made a steeple with his hands, deep in thought.

Elenna put her lips close to Tom's ear. "I hope you know what you're doing."

So do I, Tom thought.

The Judge looked up, his mouth a grim straight line. "Very well," he said. "Deliver Kensa to us, and the defendant's debt is paid."

Tom heard Aduro draw a sharp breath.

"Thank you," Tom said, bowing.

"But," said the Judge, his mouth twisting into a smile, "there's one condition."

CHAPTER THREE

FIGHTING WITH ONE ARM TIED

Tom didn't like the look of the Judge's sneer.

"What is the condition?" asked Elenna.

The Judge rubbed his hands together. "Well, you may be able to bring us Kensa – though I doubt it. But that does not excuse your intrusion on a sacred trial. There is a price you must pay for this." He pointed to the jewelled belt at Tom's waist. "Hand over your magical tokens."

Tom gasped. "I can't. I won these tokens on a Quest."

"You will," The Judge snarled. "Those magical tokens were created by Wizards, so they belong here. They're the perfect insurance to make sure you stick to your task."

"But without them the Quest will be even harder!" said Elenna.

"This is the only deal we're offering," said the Judge.

Aduro shook his head, looking straight at Tom. "It's too dangerous for you to take on Kensa without your belt."

Tom shared a look with Elenna. His friend gave a determined nod.

What choice do we have?

Slowly, Tom unclipped his belt and

dropped it to the ground at his feet. As he did so, he remembered the ruby that was still tucked in his tunic. He held his breath. Would the Judge notice?

"Aren't you forgetting something?" asked the Judge.

Tom was about to take out the red jewel, when the Judge reached into his baggy sleeve and drew out his

wand. It was made of some sort of
blackened wood, and forked at the
end. From a tassel of gold thread
hung what looked like a dragon-scale.
The shield on Tom's arm suddenly
became heavy as a bolt of silver light
struck its surface.

"Oh no!" said Elenna. "The Beast
tokens!"

Tom looked at the face of his shield,

and saw that his six magical Beast tokens had turned grey and cracked, like broken stone.

"What did you do?" he demanded.

The Judge grinned. "I've drained your tokens of their magic. You will not be able to cheat on this Quest, like you have the others."

Tom stared at the shield. It had kept him safe in so many battles and he'd called on the tokens' power countless times. How could he meet Kensa without their protection?

"Now, son of Taladon," said the Judge, "you are ready."

Despair crept over Tom's heart. *I've never felt less ready.*

Two bolts of silver shot from the wand's tip, and the courtroom vanished. Tom found himself back in Hugo's throne room, but now the

King's face looked even more worried than before.

"Did you find what you wanted?" he asked in a grave voice.

Tom and Elenna shared a glance. "Aduro's alive, at least," he said. "But we have to fight to free him."

King Hugo nodded. "I know you'll do the right thing, Tom," he said, getting up from his throne. He started to leave, when he turned round to glance towards them one last time. "Be careful on this Quest. Remember, you don't have Aduro's help this time."

Later that day, Tom stood in his bedchamber, packing Storm's saddlebags. He sheathed his sword, the blade freshly sharpened on the grinder's wheel. He'd need his sword skills more than ever now so many other powers had been taken away. Daltec had retired to Aduro's chamber to search for anything else that might help them.

A fist pounded the door twice and before Tom could say "Enter", in strode King Hugo. Tom dropped to his knee. "Your Majesty!"

The King pulled him up. "There's no need for that," he said. "You've served Avantia better than anyone else."

"Thank you," said Tom. "I only hope to serve it once more by defeating Kensa and restoring Aduro to his rightful place."

King Hugo looked around nervously and lowered his voice. "I've always known the Judge to be strict, but I never thought he was capable of something like this."

Tom nodded. "I've been thinking

about what happened," he said. "Is it possible he has some other motive? Could he be jealous of Aduro?"

King Hugo shrugged. "It's possible. Aduro is the only Wizard in the Circle who might be more powerful than him. And power can corrupt – even if it is power that you don't have."

"So the Judge wins whatever happens," said Tom. "If I bring them Kensa, he can claim the credit."

"And if you don't," muttered the King, "then Aduro is expelled from the Circle, and the Judge will finally be the most powerful Wizard of all." He reached inside the pocket of his robe and drew out what looked like a broken shard of mirror. "Aduro left this behind my throne," he said. "I think he anticipated something bad might happen."

"What is it?" asked Tom, taking the glass fragment. Its edges were worn smooth and he felt the magic running through it like an invisible current.

"Aduro showed me once, years ago," said Hugo. "It's a tracking glass. Anyone you want to find, it will show you where they are. It only works for a short time, though, so you must use its power wisely."

"Thank you," he said, stowing the shard in Storm's saddlebag.

He heard footsteps on the stairs and Elenna burst in, her bow over one shoulder and quiver strapped to her back. "Are you—" The sight of the King drew her up short and she bowed quickly. "Are you ready, Tom?"

"I'm ready," he said. "Let's get to the stables and fetch Storm and Silver."

He was halfway to the door when his shield hummed on his arm. Sepron's tooth, still grey, was rattling in the wood.

"What does it mean?" said King Hugo.

"The Sea Serpent must be in trouble," said Tom. "But this can't be happening now. I have to find Kensa!"

As they headed out to the courtyard to fetch Storm and Silver, they met Daltec struggling the other way. Under one arm he held a mahogany chest, and in his other hand he clutched a scroll.

He set the chest down clumsily and handed the scroll to Elenna. "It's a map of the kingdom," he said. "It will tell you where evil lurks."

"We know our way around Avantia now," Elenna said, opening it up.

The scroll was blank.

Elenna frowned. "Are you sure you picked up the right...."

Before she'd finished her sentence, an image formed above the parchment, floating in mid-air. A map, but unlike any Tom had ever seen. The landscape was built in three dimensions, like a tiny model. He made out the thrusting peaks of Avantia's northern mountains, the soaring summit of the Stonewin Volcano – even the towers of King Hugo's castle. The Winding River flowed like a serpent through the countryside. One part of the map was glowing brighter than the rest – the Western shore.

"That's where we're going first," said Tom. "We can help Sepron while we chase Kensa and Sanpao."

"And take this," said Daltec. He unhooked a chain from his neck, looped through what looked like a grey pebble pendant. "It's a warning stone. The last thing Aduro was working on before he was arrested. It will glow red when you are close to Sanpao and Kensa."

Tom lowered his head to let Daltec place the chain over his neck. "What's in the box?"

"Ah!" said Daltec, looking pleased with himself. "Aduro sent me to the vaults for these as soon as he knew Kensa was back." He placed

the box on the ground and began
fiddling with the catches. "They'll be
invaluable on your Quest."

"Yes, but what are they?" asked
Elenna.

Daltec unhooked the final catch and
placed a hand under the rim. He looked
at them with a twinkle in his eye.
"They're Lightning Tokens!" he said, and
flipped open the lid. Tom peered in.

The box was empty.

CHAPTER FOUR

THE PIRATE RETURNS

"Oh no!" cried the apprentice. "They've been stolen!"

"Perhaps you just misplaced them?" Elenna suggested.

Daltec shook his head, looking crestfallen. "No, I'm certain they were here."

Tom placed his hand on the young Wizard's back. He didn't like to think about what it meant if things were being stolen from under the nose of his friend. Evil was in every corner of the kingdom.

"We have to get going," he told Daltec. "Sepron might be in grave danger. Can you magic us to the Western Shore? We'll leave Storm and Silver here, for now. They won't be much use if we have to go out to sea."

"Very well," said Daltec. "Let's hope I can at least get this right."

The apprentice closed his eyes and muttered a few words under his breath. The courtyard vanished and Tom felt a shudder travel through his body. He found himself standing on hard-packed sand. Elenna was beside him, the sea breeze whipping her hair around her face. The grey sea was choppy.

Tom noticed a red glow under her tunic. "The warning stone!" he said.

Elenna tugged out the pendant, which burned bright like an ember. "Kensa and Sanpao must be close!"

Tom focused the power of the golden helmet and scanned up and down the beach. At least the Judge had left the magic of the Golden Armour intact. The Armour was kept at the Palace, but Tom didn't have to wear it to call upon its powers.

"Can you see anything?" asked Elenna.

Tom's eyes picked up a shape floating in the shallows, just beneath a distant headland. He could see a crew of stick-thin pirates in ragged clothes scampering over the decks and rigging.

"It's Sanpao's ship," he said grimly. "Kensa must be with him."

"Perhaps that's got something to do with Sepron being in trouble," said Elenna.

"Let's see what they're up to," said Tom.

They ran along the top of the beach, weaving in and out of the grassy dunes to keep hidden. Soon the huge pirate ship loomed before them. From the cracked timbers of its hull and sun-parched sails, Tom saw it was in need of repair. Sailors were daubing the timbers with tar to make her watertight, and others were hoisting patched sails and winding ropes.

"We can climb up there," said Tom, nodding towards the anchor chain that disappeared into the water. Together, they swam as quietly as possible through the shallow water, and reached the seaweed-tangled chain. Tom went first, pulling himself up, hand over hand, over the slimy metal links until he clambered, dripping, onto the weather deck. He helped

Elenna over the ship's rail and they crept behind two barrels.

Tom heard a voice he recognised.

"Next time leave the navigation to me, you great oaf," said Kensa. "You never could tell left from right."

"It's 'port' and 'starboard', dearest mistress," replied Sanpao.

Tom looked at Elenna in bewilderment, and then peered out. Up on the quarterdeck, the

Pirate King and the Sorceress of Henkrall stood on either side of the great wheel, glaring at one another. Tattoos rippled over Sanpao's bare chest, and his oiled hair, plaited with spikes, hung down his back. Kensa, as always, wore a dark cape down to the soles of her leather boots. Gold and silver threads picked out strange symbols over her robe – swirls and spirals, lightning bolts and cogs.

"Besides, it's my ship," said Sanpao. "The crew wouldn't accept a woman being in charge."

"If it weren't for this woman," sneered Kensa, "you'd still be rotting in King Hugo's dungeon."

Sanpao shook a fist at her. "For the hundredth time, I had an escape plan!"

Kensa raised her eyebrows in disbelief. "Admit it – Taladon's brat

got the better of you."

"That little urchin!" roared Sanpao. "I'll feed him to the sharks!"

Kensa placed a hand on Sanpao's muscular tattooed arm. "It won't be long. The Lightning Beasts are free of their prison now."

Tom felt Elenna's fingers grip his shoulder. *What are the Lightning Beasts?*

"We need to deal with the brat first," said Sanpao. "He's got a knack for coming to the rescue."

Kensa tipped back her head and laughed. "Not this time, Sanpao. The only way to defeat the Lightning Beasts is with the Lightning Tokens."

"And?" said Sanpao.

Kensa reached beneath her long cloak and drew out a leather bag, attached to her waist with a strand of rope. "And Tom does not have them," she cackled. "We do."

Sanpao turned from the wheel and bellowed at his crew: "Anchor away!"

Pirates leapt to their duties across the deck, and Tom heard the rattle of the anchor being drawn up.

"Quicker, you stinking scallywags!" screeched Kensa.

Weary-looking pirates shimmied up

the rigging to unfurl the sails. With a creak of ropes, the ship lurched across the water.

"We need a plan to get those tokens," said Elenna, as the vessel climbed out of the waves and into the sky. Even though Tom had seen the magical ship many times, he still had to swallow back a gasp.

"Can you distract the crew?" he said. "I'll deal with Kensa."

Elenna nodded, then darted across the deck and scrambled up the mast of the ship. One by one, with cries of alarm, the pirate crew spotted her.

Good work! thought Tom

"Catch that girl!" roared Sanpao. The other sailors drew their cutlasses and swarmed towards the mast. Tom waited until he was sure Kensa was looking at Elenna too, then crept from behind the barrel and up to the quarterdeck. As he drew his sword, it made a sound. Kensa spun around.

"You!" she said.

With a deft flick of his wrist, Tom severed the leather bag from Kensa's waist and caught it.

"Taladon's brat is here!" she cried, pulling a whip from her robe. It was studded with shards of broken glass, and Tom had to duck as it lashed over his head. He heard a low thunk, and saw that it had wrapped around the mast. Kensa struggled to free it.

Sanpao spun around and drew his curved blade. "I'll chop you so fine the crabs won't even have to chew," he snarled. The rest of the sailors left the mast and climbed the steps to the quarterdeck.

Too many to face alone, thought Tom, backing to the ship's rail.

Tom heard a twang and saw Elenna

swinging towards him on a rope.
"Grab me!" she cried.

Tom reached out and gripped her waist
as she swung past. His feet left the deck,
and they swung through the air. Together
they plummeted towards the sea.

CHAPTER FIVE

BODIES IN THE WATER

Tom and Elenna slammed into the water. For a moment he choked in a torrent of bubbles, and then he felt his body rising, rising, rising. Finally, his head broke the surface and he took in great gasps of air. Elenna was beside him in the freezing sea, doing the same. Tom looked up – Sanpao's ship was descending and the pirates

65

had gathered by the deck-rails. Already they were levelling their mighty crossbows and winding the mechanisms.

"Loose!" roared Sanpao. The first bolt, a shaft of sharpened whalebone, stabbed into the water a sword-length from Tom and Elenna.

"We're sitting ducks!" said Tom.

"No, we're not," cried Elenna. "Look!"

Tom turned and saw rainbow scales breaking the water a hundred paces to his left. Then a crested head rolled into view.

"Sepron!" Tom shouted in relief, just as Kensa's voice shrieked: "Again!"

The Sea Serpent dipped under the waves and glided beneath them. Tom and Elenna were scooped up in the Good Beast's coils and placed gently

on his back. Before the second pirate
missile hit the water, they'd surged
away. Sepron cut through the waves
faster than any ship, and salty spray
scattered in his wake. Soon Sanpao's
vessel shrank to a distant dot in the
sky.

"Once things have calmed down, we should go back and fight them," said Tom, tying the bag of tokens to his waist.

"There were too many," said Elenna behind him.

Tom's frustration burned. They had to capture Kensa for the Circle of Wizards if Aduro was ever to be freed. He tried to use the ruby to tell Sepron to stop, but it was no use.

"He's heading away from Avantia," Tom said. "Where's he taking us?"

"Maybe he knows something about those Lightning Beasts Kensa mentioned," said Elenna.

"Or maybe he's taking us there!" Tom gasped, pointing ahead.

A smudge of land had appeared on the horizon to the west.

"I don't understand. There

shouldn't be any land there," said
Elenna. "Gwildor is at least a two-day
voyage away."

"It can't be Gwildor, can it?" said
Tom. But as they came closer, he
recognised the bright colours of the
Gwildorian jungle.

Tom felt a chill across his skin.
Kensa had mentioned Beasts torn
from their Lightning Prisons. Was this
strange land movement connected
to the use of forbidden Lightning
Magic? He took the scroll map from
inside his tunic, expecting it to be
soaked through, but somehow it had
remained intact – and it had changed.
Off the Western Shore of Avantia,
across a very short expanse of ocean,
lay the land of Gwildor.

"It's too close," Tom muttered. "We
shouldn't be able to see Gwildor and

Avantia in the same map."

Right before his eyes, the map shifted and the kingdoms moved closer still. A word wrote itself over the shrunken ocean: *Solak*.

"Solak must be the name of the first Lightning Beast," said Tom, his eyes scanning the sea around them. "We need to be—"

His voice died when he saw a lifeless form in the water ahead of him – a mighty red shell floating in the waves.

"Krabb!" Elenna gasped. "Is he… dead?"

The Beast's legs hung limply in the water. Now Tom understood why Sepron had ignored their requests to turn back.

He felt his chest tighten in fear. If Krabb was dead, what about

Gwildor's Mistress of the Beasts?

Tom's heart pounded against his ribs as he spied an armoured figure lying motionless on Krabb's wide shell. "Mother?" he croaked.

Sepron surged faster towards the lifeless bodies.

Please, don't be dead, Tom willed.
Just move to show me you're alive.

Sepron drew up alongside Krabb. Tom hopped from one Beast to the other, crouching at Freya's side. She lay on her front, her face was pale and hair sodden. Tom saw no blood on her clothes, or on Krabb's shell. He found Freya's wrist and felt for a pulse. It was weak, but he could feel one.

"She's alive!" he called to Elenna. As he rolled his mother over, she winced. *She might have broken ribs*, he thought. *Or a fracture in her arm*. He eased her back down gently and her eyelids flickered open.

She gave a weak smile. "Tom?"

"You're safe now," he said.

Freya's face turned serious.
"No… Evil Beast… In the water…"

"You must rest," Tom said.

"Healing token," Freya said in a whisper. "At my waist."

Tom reached into the leather pouch that was around his mother's middle. He found what he was looking for – a curious leaf the same shade of green as one of the tokens taken from his belt. If he was right, it should have the power to heal. He held it over his mother's ribs.

"Krabb first," she muttered, but Tom ignored her. Slowly, a smile of comfort spread across her lips as she struggled to sit up. "Thank you."

Tom next took out the Pearl of Gwildor, which allowed whoever held it to breathe underwater. He stood up, unhooking his sword and shield and handing them to Elenna. "I'll be back in a moment," he said. Clutching the pearl and the leaf, he dived into the water. The cold wrapped around him like a cloak of ice, but he swam down quickly to warm himself.

The water was clear, and Tom could see instantly that three of Krabb's legs were swaying at awkward angles. *They're broken!* Swimming between them, and holding the leaf to the wounds, he watched the shattered sections of shell fuse together. He looked and saw another wound, this time a shallow gash in Krabb's soft belly.

What sort of creature could have caused such damage? he wondered.

A shadow fell over Tom, and he jerked around. The biggest shark he had ever seen drifted through the water twenty paces away. Its skin was pale blue, with patches of purple that seemed to spread and vanish in an instant. Its fins seemed to be made

up of spiked bone blades. Its glassy
eyes were deep black, filled with hate
and fixed on Tom. The Shark-Beast's
mouth parted to reveal hundreds of
teeth trailing scraps of bloodied flesh.

He knew in a heartbeat that this
was...Solak, the first Lightning Beast!

CHAPTER SIX

RACE TO THE SHORE

I'm underwater without any weapons, facing a Beast that's so strong that he almost killed Krabb! Tom thought.

He stowed the Pearl of Gwildor in his tunic, and kicked for the surface. As soon as he broke through, he pointed and called out: "A Beast!"

Elenna reached out a hand and helped Tom scramble up onto Krabb's shell. Water showered over them as Solak burst from the sea. His skin darkened to indigo as his head rose above the surface, mouth gaping to reveal deadly teeth. Elenna swung Tom's sheathed sword, smashing the Beast across his nose. Solak veered away, but quickly turned for another attack, churning up white foamy waves with his powerful, lashing tail. Tom had to grip the shell to keep from sliding off.

"Hold tight!" yelled Freya. "I'll get us to safety." She let out a series of high-pitched squeals, unlike any sound Tom had heard before. Krabb's eyes swivelled, and Gwildor's Master of the Sea surged towards the shoreline.

For a moment, Tom saw no sign of Solak, but then the Lightning Beast's bone-fin broke the water. It cut through the ocean in pursuit, faster than a horse at full gallop. His skin flickered violet, then navy, then pale blue again.

"He's gaining!" Elenna cried.

Freya urged Krabb with another clicking squeak and the Good Beast responded with a surge of speed.

Will Krabb's healed legs be enough to help us escape Kensa's creature? Tom wondered, as he quickly strapped on his sword and shield.

Looking back over his shoulder, Tom stared right into Solak's hungry black eyes. The Lightning Beast scythed through the waves after them. The gap became smaller, and still land was far away. Solak gave a jerk of his tail, and propelled himself out of the sea. His mouth opened,

showing an array of teeth as he shot
through the air towards them. Tom
drew his sword and swung. The blade
rang out as it shattered the bottom
of Solak's jaws, sending his teeth
scattering like shards of rock. Tom
covered his face as several bounced
around him, off Krabb's shell and
into the sea.

"Got you!" he shouted.

The Beast crashed back into the waves with a snarl, only to reappear a heartbeat later. When he opened his mouth, Tom's heart sank. The teeth had already regrown! The shark's eyes flashed in anger.

This Beast is tough! But Avantia and Aduro are relying on us...

Tom leant out as far as he dared and slammed his shield into Solak's nose. The Beast dipped beneath the surface once more, and then snapped his head up quickly, gripping the shield with his teeth and shaking his head from side to side.

Tom felt himself losing his balance as the Beast thrashed.

"You have to let go!" Elenna cried. Tom tried again to heave his shield free, but Solak whipped it from his arm, almost pulling Tom's shoulder out of its socket. Tom fell to his knees with a gasp of pain and watched in dismay as the Beast dived, taking the shield with him.

"No!" he shouted.

Elenna's eyes widened as she noticed his missing shield.

"We have to go back," Tom said.

Freya shook her head and pointed to the approaching shoreline. "We've nearly reached safety. We should regroup and make a plan."

Tom scrabbled to the edge of Krabb's shell, drawing his sword.

"What are you doing?" asked Elenna.

"I don't have my belt anymore," Tom replied. "I can't lose my shield, too."

He was about to jump, but felt

himself being pulled backwards.
He landed hard on his back across
Krabb's shell.

"I won't let you get yourself killed,"
said Elenna, standing over him.

Solak's nose broke the surface
again, showering them with spray.

As Tom struggled to his feet, Elenna
hooked two arrows to her bowstring
and shot them. The arrowheads
thumped into the Beast's flank but
he hardly slowed down.

He's angry, thought Tom, *and he
wants to finish us off. Well, I'll give him
a fight first.*

As he brandished his sword, a shape
appeared in the waves to Solak's left.
Tom recognised the crested green
snout at once. "Sepron!"

Avantia's Sea Serpent arced above
the water, and his long shadow fell

over Solak. The Evil Beast slowed, his skin going almost white. He had nowhere to go. Sepron's body crashed on top of him, sending up a wall of seawater that almost knocked Tom, Elenna and Freya off Krabb's back.

For a few moments the water was still. Tom saw the seabed clearly beneath them as Krabb floated into

84

the shallows close to the Gwildorian shore.

"Solak has to be dead," said Elenna. "Nothing could survive that blow."

Sepron's rainbow scales flashed past a little further out and his head lifted above the waves.

"Thank you!" Tom called.

But the Sea Serpent wasn't looking at him. The slits of his green eyes were facing out to sea. Tom followed the Beast's gaze, and saw a bone-fin cutting through the water, moving away from them.

"The Scourge of the Sea isn't finished yet," said Freya, watching.

As Krabb clambered onto the beach, Freya jumped from his shell, with Tom and Elenna not far behind. *When Solak returns, we'll be ready*, Tom thought.

CHAPTER SEVEN

A NEW PLAN

A little while later, the three of them sat on the beach, huddled around a fire. Tom's tunic was almost dry, and after a meal of freshly caught fish their stomachs were full. But nothing else was right. While they ate, Tom and Elenna had filled Freya in on everything that had happened since they last saw her, at Taladon's funeral.

Now, Tom's gaze drifted to the

ocean. Krabb was patrolling the
shallows, swimming back and forth.
Beyond him lay Avantia's coast, a
distant smudge on the horizon. Tom
knew that Sepron would be guarding
the seas there too. But somewhere
between the two Good Beasts lurked
the deadly Solak.

"I can't believe I've lost my shield,"

said Tom, thumping the sand.
"I was so stupid!"

Elenna placed another piece
of wood on the fire. "You were
protecting us," she said. "We'll
get you another shield."

Tom picked up the despair in her
voice. They both knew his shield
wasn't just a piece of wood. Ancient
wizards had carved it from the Tree
of Being. It had saved Tom's life more
times than he could remember, and
now it lay somewhere on the seabed
of the Western Ocean.

Freya stood up and grimaced in
pain. She picked up her sword.

"Mother," said Tom. "Your injuries
have not fully healed. You cannot—"

"If what you've told me is right,"
said Freya, interrupting him, "then
the Lightning Beasts are threatening

the balance of the kingdoms. That's why the lands are shifting."

"And in that case," said Tom, "I will deal with them."

"No," said Freya. "You must fulfil your promise to the Circle of Wizards and find Kensa. I will protect the kingdoms."

Tom looked at his mother and the determined look on her face.

She's tackled countless Beasts, he thought, *but perhaps this is one Quest too far.*

"I won't let you battle Solak alone," he said. "Any Beast that can almost kill Krabb and withstand an attack from Sepron is too much for one warrior."

"I think the Lightning Magic has destroyed the natural order of things and weakened the Good Beasts," Freya said.

"That means the kingdoms are more vulnerable than ever," said Elenna.

Guilt settled heavily in Tom's stomach. *If I hadn't let Kensa get into Avantia, none of this would have happened. It's my fault the Lightning Beasts are free.*

Elenna must have read the look on his face. She touched his arm and leant closer. "There's nothing else you could have done," he said. "Kensa would have destroyed Henkrall and Avantia if we hadn't pursued her."

"But now the threat to Avantia is even greater," Tom said, standing up and strapping on his sword. As he did, his hand found the sack at his waist. He'd almost forgotten it was there – the bag he'd liberated from Kensa on Sanpao's ship. He opened the cord and, crouching, poured out

the contents onto the sand. Six glass
balls of various colours, each the size
of a large marble.

"What are those?" asked his
mother.

"Lightning tokens," said Tom.
"They're supposed to help us defeat
the Beasts, but I can't see what good
they could do." He held a green one
closer to his face and saw the tiny
symbol of a lightning fork, seemingly
floating inside the orb.

"Kensa obviously thought they were powerful," said Elenna. "Otherwise, why would she have stolen them?"

Tom stowed the tokens away and retied the bag. Magic or not, he felt ready to carry on with his new mission. Solak might have taken his shield from him, but no Beast could take his spirit. *While there's blood in my veins, no Quest is impossible.*

"Call Krabb," he said. "We're going fishing for a shark!"

CHAPTER EIGHT

GHOST OF TALADON

Krabb emerged from the sea, his mighty claws carving up the sand as he approached. When he reached them, the Beast lowered his massive body to the ground.

Tom climbed onto his shell, and held out a hand to pull Elenna up beside him. Freya placed a foot on one of Krabb's legs, ready to jump aboard. She winced as she moved.

Tom drew a breath. "You need to stay here," he said.

Freya frowned. "I'm fine."

"You're still weak," he replied. "I can't let you put your life at risk."

Freya's lips formed a tight line. "I'm Gwildor's Mistress of the Beasts. This is my fight."

"Freya," Elenna said gently, "your kingdom needs you alive, not dead. It's obvious you're still in pain. Let us tackle Solak. If we fail, you can take on the Quest."

Freya's face was grave, but she nodded and stepped back from Krabb. "Promise me you will both be careful."

Tom tapped the sword-hilt at his waist. "It's Solak who needs to be afraid," he said. He rapped his

knuckles on Krabb's shell and the
Beast straightened up. Then he began
to step back towards the shallows.

"Wait!" Freya called. "You might
need this." She threw the gleaming
Pearl of Gwildor towards them.

Elenna caught it, and stowed it in her tunic. "Thank you!"

Krabb carried them out to sea and soon Freya was just a distant figure on the shoreline. *I hope we don't regret going on alone*, thought Tom.

The daylight began to fade as the sun set. Tom and Elenna sat back to back, scanning the water for any sign of Solak.

Even with the power of the golden helmet, Tom couldn't see far into the murky depths. He thought of Aduro, languishing in a dank cell. The bargain he had struck with the Judge was beginning to feel foolish. *We can't even begin to hunt Kensa and fulfil our deal with the Judge until all six Beasts are defeated! But Aduro would understand. He knows that the fate of the kingdoms is the most important thing.*

Krabb stopped suddenly, and Tom saw a wave, larger than the others, lap against the Good Beast's shell. He glanced over to where the wave had come from and spotted what looked like a flash of white, then blue.

Solak!

Sure enough, the bone fin rose out of the waves again – closer this time – then vanished.

"He's heading this way," said Elenna, reaching for her quiver

Tom scanned the horizon. "Where have you gone?" he muttered.

Krabb suddenly lurched in the water and let out a strange growl. Tom saw the huge dark shadow of Solak pass silent and deadly beneath them. The shark-Beast turned and came for another pass. Again, Krabb juddered. Elenna fell into Tom and

they clutched each other to stay
steady.

"What's happening?" Elenna asked,
as an angry Krabb slapped the water
with his pincers.

Tom spotted a cloud of red blood
drifting from beneath them. Suddenly
he understood. "Solak's slashing
Krabb's belly with his bone-fin!
I should have known – that's how
he was injured before!"

Solak surged past again. Tom felt
a shudder of fear run through his
own body when he noticed blood
spreading across the water in dark
swirls. He seized the red jewel and
hoped Krabb could understand:
Head back to shore!

All he felt in return was Krabb's
helpless pain, until another voice
intruded. Tom felt as though the

words were stabbing into his head, jagged and angry:

Son… Taladon… Die…

"Solak's speaking to me!" he told Elenna.

Die…Die…Die… The words fell like ringing blows, making Tom feel dizzy. He gripped his temples and crumpled to his knees. Elenna came to kneel beside him, keeping her arrow trained on the water.

"What is it, Tom?" she gasped.

He could barely answer. "The Beast hates me… He wants me dead."

Suddenly, Solak launched himself out of the waves, rows of teeth snapping. Droplets of water scattered from his muscular body as his bone-fin sliced the air. Elenna leapt up and loosed her arrow straight into the Beast's mouth. Solak's glassy eyes

widened and he gave a choking roar, dropping back into the bloody water with a massive splash that nearly threw them off Krabb's shell.

The arrow must have stunned him, because for a moment the angry thoughts stopped attacking Tom's mind, the pain in his head retreating. Tom found his feet again, waiting for Solak to re-emerge. From the depths a message came, clearer than before.

It was unmistakeable. Tom repeated the words under his breath:

"The son of Taladon must die."

CHAPTER NINE

EASY PREY

The darkening sky was bruised with clouds, and Tom heard a low rumble rattle the air.

"A thunderstorm," said Elenna. "Perhaps it has something to do with the Lightning Beast."

Solak emerged from the water to Tom's right, so he threw himself across Krabb's shell. As the shark-Beast opened his terrible jaws to bite Krabb's

105

leg, Tom swung his sword, stabbing deep into the Beast's red throat. Solak roared and clamped his jaw shut over the blade.

"Not again!" cried Tom, trying to free it. Solak's black eyes gleamed with triumph as he wrenched his head to and fro. Tom gasped in pain as his arm jolted and jerked. *This time I'm not letting go!* he promised himself. *And I'm not going to die...*

Elenna leapt to his side and shot arrow after arrow into Solak's head. Each one lodged in the mottled blue flesh, leaving trails of blood, but they did nothing to stop him. The new wounds seemed to make Solak even more furious, and he thrashed about with greater energy. At last Tom managed to pull his sword free, but his foot slipped off the edge of the shell.

With a cry, he toppled off Krabb's back
and across Solak's neck.

Lightning flashed across the sky,
brighter. Thunder grumbled, louder.
The storm is very close now, Tom realised.

Solak dived, and Tom slid sideways.

He reached out and his hand grasped something. He hissed as searing pain shot through his palm. The bone-fin! Tom gritted his teeth against the pain, and made himself hold on as Solak plunged.

He didn't even have time to suck in a breath before he went under. As his lungs began to burn, he remembered that Elenna had the Pearl that would allow him to survive beneath the water.

The Beast rolled over and over, trying to shake Tom loose. He sheathed his sword and gripped the fin with both hands. It eased the pain a fraction, but now he wasn't able to fight. As they dived deeper, water streamed up his nostrils and pressed against his eardrums.

I'm totally at the Beast's mercy!

Solak descended to the boulder-encrusted seabed and turned over as he swam, trying to bash Tom off his flank. Seaweed whipped past Tom's face, but he clung on. Then a rock caught him square on the shoulder, and threw him loose. Solak streaked away.

He hasn't noticed I've gone, thought Tom. This was his moment to escape. He needed time to think about his next plan of action.

He spotted the silhouette of Krabb's body above and struck out for the surface, desperate to breathe. When he broke through the waves, he sucked in grateful gasps, even through a barrage of rain that pounded his face. The storm had grown worse.

"Thank goodness!" said Elenna, kneeling on Krabb's shell and reaching out. "Quick, get on! Whoa!" Elenna flinched as a fork of lightning lit up the sky above them.

Of course! Tom thought, feeling for the bag at his waist. *The Tokens!* "Lightning tokens to fight Lightning Beasts," he said.

"What are you waiting for?" asked Elenna, through the lashing rain. "Solak will be coming for you."

Tom grinned. "Hand me the Pearl."

Elenna frowned, but did as he asked. He untied his sword and tossed it to her.

"I don't like this," she said.

Tom looked up at the churning sky. "I've got a plan," he said, "but I need Solak to think I'm defenceless."

"Without your sword or shield," said Elenna, "you *are* defenceless!"

"Not quite," said Tom.

He reached into the sack at his waist

and searched among the tokens. Which one could be used against Solak? He drew out one of the tokens – a blue orb. *Blue for a water Beast? I hope so.*

He rolled forwards and kicked towards the depths. He couldn't see the Scourge of the Sea anywhere, but he knew Solak waited somewhere nearby. With the pearl in one hand, Tom didn't have to worry about running out of breath. He struggled to see through the mist of Krabb's blood, but he knew the Beast's nose would have no problem finding him. Solak could surely smell an easy meal.

Well, come and get me, Tom thought.

He let his body go limp in the water, pretending to be severely injured or dead. Part of his mind screamed at him to swim away, but Tom kept calm.
I know what I'm doing. There's no other way to defeat this Beast.

CHAPTER TEN

THE POWER OF LIGHTNING

He didn't have long to wait. Through hooded eyes, Tom glimpsed Solak nosing through the water above. But the shark-Beast was swimming lazily towards the injured Krabb. That wasn't part of the plan! Tom shifted slightly in the water and Solak's nose twitched as he picked up the blood-scent. Then his eyes rolled downwards, fixing on Tom.

With a flick of his muscular tail, he veered off course and headed towards him.

Tom ignored his thumping heart. He needed to wait until the last possible moment to put his plan into action. *If Solak realises it's a trap, it's not only me in danger. Elenna and Krabb will be left at the mercy of the Lightning Beast. And if we fail, Aduro will never be set free...*

Solak put on a burst of speed, his mouth snapping hungrily. Tom tensed his muscles, ready to dodge. At five paces away, Solak's black eyes rolled back in his head and he bared his jagged teeth. Tom cast the Lightning Token towards the Beast's gaping mouth and watched it arc between Solak's razor-sharp teeth to knock against his gums before disappearing down his throat.

I did it!

He turned to swim away, but felt himself pulled backwards. One of the shark-Beast's teeth had snagged on his tunic. With a jerk of his head, Solak dragged Tom inside his mouth.

Darkness fell all around him as the Beast's mouth clamped shut. Tom closed his eyes tight, waiting for the tips of teeth to pierce his flesh. But after a moment, he dared to peer out again. He wasn't dead. Somehow Solak's jagged teeth hadn't ripped him to shreds! His tunic had torn free and

a wave of water must have pushed him deeper into the giant mouth.

I'm trapped inside a Beast!

He saw the Lightning Token lodged behind a tooth, giving out a faint blue glow. As he swam towards it, he felt a strange sucking all over his body, drawing him deeper into the Beast's throat. He grabbed at the base of a tooth, and seized the Lightning Token too, but the suction grew stronger. The muscles of Solak's gullet gripped him like a vice.

Tom let go of the Token and watched it plummet into the depths of the Beast's throat. He gripped the tooth with both hands, fighting to hold on.

It's over, he thought. *I'm going to be eaten alive by Solak!*

BOOM!

Tom squeezed his eyes shut as a

shockwave pressed in from every side. He felt himself rolling over and over. When he opened his eyes again, Solak's body had vanished, replaced with thousands of blue bubbles. All that remained was the bone-fin, floating to the seabed.

The Lightning Token must have exploded!

Tom swam towards the surface through the cascading bubbles – all that remained of the Scourge of the Sea. He made sure the other tokens were still secure at his waist.

Elenna was right – Daltec didn't let us down.

Tom's head broke the surface. The storm was passing, and only a light drizzle now fell. He saw Elenna, still on Krabb's back, punch the air in delight. She pointed at something floating on the waves to Tom's left.

"My shield!" he cried. It must have been in Solak's stomach, too.

Tom retrieved it, and then swam over to Krabb. He gratefully accepted Elenna's hand. "I thought you were shark food," she said.

"I sort of was," Tom replied, once he

was safely up. "I had to get right inside his mouth."

Standing up on Krabb's back, he looked towards Avantia.

"Is it just me?" he asked his friend, "or does it seem further away already?"

"It does," said Elenna, smiling.

Tom felt a glimmer of hope. He hated to think what would have happened if Gwildor and Avantia had collided.

Turning around, he saw Freya waving from the shore of Gwildor. Using the golden helmet Tom could see the beaming smile on his mother's face. But he was troubled. Could she tell him why Solak had been so determined to kill the son of Taladon? How did this Beast even know who his father was? He rubbed Krabb's shell.

"Take us to shore, brave friend."

"Where's the next Beast?" Elenna asked, as Krabb swam weakly back towards the beach.

Tom took out the scroll from his tunic. Again, it remained bone-dry. It magically sprang to life when he unrolled it. But something wasn't right. For, although the shores of Avantia and Gwildor were indeed moving apart in the south, a great shelf of land had appeared in the north.

And it was moving closer to both kingdoms.

"There must be more evil magic at work," said Tom.

The map shuddered and shifted with tiny earthquakes as the lands crunched together. Mountain ranges thrust into the sky as they watched.

Tom swallowed as he recognised the landscape of the strange kingdom that had joined Avantia and Gwildor. He saw the Golden Valley, the Icy Desert, and the towers of Meaton, the capital city.

"Unless I'm mistaken," he said, "that's Kayonia, the World of Chaos."

Elenna frowned and peered closer. "Yes...but how?"

Tom put away the map and gazed at the horizon. Although the storm had lifted, and the dusk sky was clear and star-filled, Tom knew that the worlds were far from peaceful. If Kayonia could come to Avantia, anything was possible.

Unless we tackle the other five Beasts soon, all three kingdoms are doomed.

Join Tom on the next stage
of the Beast Quest when he meets

KAJIN
THE BEAST CATCHER

Win an exclusive
east Quest T-shirt and goody bag!

m has battled many fearsome Beasts and we want to know
ich one is your favourite! Send us a drawing or painting of
ur favourite Beast and tell us in 30 words why you think
it's the best.

Each month we will select **three** winners to receive
a Beast Quest T-shirt and goody bag!

Send your entry on a postcard to
BEAST QUEST COMPETITION
Orchard Books, 338 Euston Road, London NW1 3BH.

Australian readers should email:
childrens.books@hachette.com.au

New Zealand readers should write to:
Beast Quest Competition, PO Box 3255, Shortland St,
Auckland 1140, NZ or email: childrensbooks@hachette.co.nz

**)on't forget to include your name and address.
Only one entry per child.**

Good luck!

Fight the Beasts,
Fear the Magic

www.beastquest.co.uk

Have you checked out the Beast Quest website?
It's the place to go for games, downloads, activities
sneak previews and lots of fun!

You can read all about your favourite beasts,
download free screensavers and desktop wallpaper
for your computer, and even challenge your friend
to a Beast Tournament.

Sign up to the newsletter at www.beastquest.co.uk
to receive exclusive extra content and the
opportunity to enter special members-only
competitions. We'll send you up-to-date info on al
the Beast Quest books, including the next exciting
series which features four brand-new Beasts!

Series 14: THE CURSED DRAGON
COLLECT THEM ALL!

Tom must face four terrifying Beasts as he searches for the ingredients for a potion to rescue the Cursed Dragon.

978 1 40832 920 7

978 1 40832 921 4

978 1 40832 922 1

978 1 40832 923 8

Join Tom on his Beast Quests
and take part in a terrifying adventure
where YOU call the shots!

Read on for an exclusive extract of
CEPHALOX THE CYBER SQUID!

THE MERRYN TOUCH

The water was up to Max's knees and still rising. Soon it would reach his waist. Then his chest. Then his face.

I'm going to die down here, he thought.

He hammered on the dome with all his strength, but the plexiglass held firm.

Then he saw something pale looming through the dark water outside the submersible. A long, silvery spike. It must be the squid-creature, with one of its weird robotic attachments. Any second now it would smash the glass and finish him off...

There was a crash. The sub rocked. The silver spike thrust through the broken plexiglass. More water surged in. Then the spike withdrew and the water poured in faster. Max forced his way against the torrent to the opening. If he could just squeeze through the gap...

The jet of water pushed him back. He took one last deep breath, and then the water was over his head.

He clamped his mouth shut, struggling forwards, feeling the pressure on his lungs build.

Something gripped his arms, but it wasn't the squid's tentacle – it was a pair of hands, pulling him through the hole. The broken plexiglass scraped his sides and then he was through.

The monster was nowhere to be seen. In the dim underwater light, he made out the face of his rescuer. It was the Merryn girl, and next to her was a large silver swordfish.

She smiled at him.

Max couldn't smile back. He'd been saved from a metal coffin, only to swap it for a watery one. The pressure of the ocean squeezed him on every side. His lungs felt as though they were bursting.

He thrashed his limbs, rising upwards. He looked to where he thought the surface was, but saw nothing, only endless water. His cheeks puffed with the effort to hold in air. He let some of it out slowly, but it only made him want to breathe in more.

He knew he had no chance. He was too deep, he'd never make it to the surface in time. Soon he'd no longer be able to hold his breath. The water would swirl into his lungs and he'd die here, at the bottom of the sea. *Just like my mother*, he thought.

The Merryn girl rose up beside him, reached out and put her hands on his neck. Warmth seemed to flow from her fingers. Then the warmth turned to pain. What was happening? It got worse and worse, until Max felt as if his throat was being ripped open. Was she trying to kill him?

———

He struggled in panic, trying to push her off. His mouth opened and water rushed in.

That was it. He was going to die.

Then he realised something – the water was cool and sweet. He sucked it down into his lungs. Nothing had ever tasted so good.

He was breathing underwater!

He put his hands to his neck and found two soft, gill-like openings where the Merryn girl had touched him. His eyes widened in astonishment.

The girl smiled.

Other strange things were happening. Max found he could see more clearly. The water seemed lighter and thinner. He made out the shapes of underwater plants, rock formations and shoals of fish in the distance, which had been invisible before. And he didn't feel as if the ocean was crushing him any more.

Is this what it's like to be a Merryn? he wondered.

"I'm Lia," said the girl. "And this is Spike." She patted the swordfish on the back and it nuzzled against her.

"Hi, I'm Max." He clapped his hand to his mouth in shock. He was speaking the same strange language of sighs and whistles he'd heard the girl use when he first met her – but now it made sense, as if he was born to speak it.

"What have you done to me?" he said.

"Saved your life," said Lia. "You're welcome, by the way."

"Oh – don't think I'm not grateful – I am. But – you've turned me into a Merryn?"

The girl laughed. "Not exactly, but I've given you some Merryn powers. You can breathe underwater, speak our language, and your senses are much stronger. Come on – we need to get away from here. The Cyber Squid may come back."

In one graceful movement she slipped onto Spike's back. Max clambered on behind her.

"Hold tight," Lia said. "Spike – let's go!"

Max put his arms around the Merryn's waist. He was jerked backwards as the swordfish shot off through the water, but he managed to hold on.

They raced above underwater forests of gently waving fronds, and hills and valleys of rock. Max saw giant crabs scuttling over the seabed. Undersea creatures loomed up – jellyfish, an octopus, a school of dolphins – but Spike nimbly swerved round them.

"Where are we going?" Max asked.

"You'll see," Lia said over her shoulder.

"I need to find my dad," Max said. The crazy things that had happened in the last few moments had driven his father from his mind. Now it all came flooding back. Was his dad gone for good? "We have to do something! That monster's got my dad – and my dogbot too!"

"It's not the Cyber Squid who wants your father. It's the Professor who's *controlling* the Cyber Squid. I tried to warn you back at the city – but you wouldn't listen."

"I didn't understand you then!"

"You Breathers don't try to understand – that's your whole problem!"

"I'm trying now. What is that monster? And who is the Professor?"

"I'll explain everything when we arrive."

"Arrive where?"

The seabed suddenly fell away. A steep valley sloped down, leading way, way deeper than the ocean ridge Aquora was built on. The swordfish dived. The water grew darker.

Far below, Max saw a faint yellow glimmer. As he watched it grew bigger and brighter, until it became a vast undersea city of golden-glinting rock rushing up towards them. There were towers, spires, domes, bridges, courtyards, squares, gardens. A city as big as Aquora, and far more beautiful, at the bottom of the sea.

———

Max gasped in amazement. The water was dark, but the city emitted a glow of its own – a warm phosphorescent light that spilled from the many windows. The rock sparkled.

Orange, pink and scarlet corals and seashells decorated the walls in intricate patterns.

"This is – amazing!" he said.

Lia turned round and smiled at him. "It's my home," she said. "Sumara!"

DARE YOU DIVE IN?

Deep in the water lurks